THE CHILDREN'S CLASSICS Collection

Dados Internacionais de Catalogação na Publicação (CIP) de acordo com ISBD

M787a Montgomery, Lucy Maud
Anne of Green Gables / Lucy Maud Montgomery. - Jandira, SP : W. Books, 2025.
128 p. : 12,80cm x 19,80cm. - (Classics).

ISBN: 978-65-5294-126-8

1. Literatura canadense. 2. Romance. 3. Canadá. 4. Imaginação. 5. Fantasia. 6. Aventura. I. Título. II. Série.

2025-2474 CDD 810
CDU 821.111(71)

Elaborada por Lucio Feitosa - CRB-8/8803
Índice para catálogo sistemático:
1. Literatura canadense 810
2. Literatura canadense 821.111(71)

Text based on the original story by L.M. Montgomery,
adapted by Gemma Barder
Illustrations by Grace Westwood

1st edition in 2025
www.cirandacultural.com.br

Anne of Green Gables

L.M. Montgomery

W. Books

Anne Shirley

An orphaned girl

Matthew and Marilla Cuthbert

A brother and sister who own Green Gables

Rachel Lynde

A family friend of
the Cuthberts

Mrs Spencer
A woman who lives
in White Sands

Gilbert Blythe
A boy who lives
in Avonlea

Diana Barry
A girl who lives
in Avonlea

Miss Stacy
A schoolteacher

Chapter One

Anne decided that if no one came to pick her up from the Avonlea train station, she would spend the night in the cherry tree on the other side of the platform. It might not be comfortable, but the view of the stars would be like no other.

Anne was so lost in this daydream that she didn't notice Matthew Cuthbert. He had arrived, taken one look at her, then turned to the station master in shock.

'But she's a girl!' said Matthew. 'We asked for a boy!'

'I don't know what to say,' said the station master. 'Mrs Spencer dropped her off saying she was to live with the Cuthberts at Green Gables. What are you going to do?'

Matthew shook his head. He wasn't good at making decisions.

He usually left that to his sister, Marilla Cuthbert. When Marilla decided that they should take on an orphaned boy to help them on their farm, Matthew had agreed. But this orphan was not a boy. She was a girl. A girl with two long red plaits, a face full of freckles and curious green eyes now turned towards him.

The sound of the two men talking had finally interrupted Anne's daydream.

Oh, I do hope that's Mr Cuthbert here to collect me, she thought, as

orphan
A child with no parents. Most commonly it is when the parents have died and a child is then taken to an orphanage.

she trotted along the platform to greet him. 'Mr Cuthbert? Of Green Gables? How do you do?' She held out her hand eagerly. Matthew shook it more cautiously.

'Is … Is that all your luggage?' he said, pointing to the small carpet bag at Anne's feet that held all her worldly possessions.

'Sure is,' said Anne. 'It isn't heavy, but if you don't carry it a certain way the handle falls off!' She lifted the bag carefully to demonstrate.

'Well then,' said Matthew. 'I suppose you ought to come along with me …'

He led Anne out of the station to his horse and wagon. He did not know what Marilla would say when he brought a girl rather than a boy back to Green Gables, but instead of making a firm decision either way, he decided to do what he so often did – he would leave the decision up to his sister.

Chapter Two

The country road from the train station to Green Gables was pretty and winding, with fields and farms beyond each hedgerow. Anne gasped with delight when she saw the sparkling waters of a lake.

'Oh, my goodness!' she cried. 'How beautiful! What does the water make you think of, Mr Cuthbert?'

Matthew was not used to talking to children. He cleared his throat and replied, 'I, er, I don't rightly know, miss.'

'A bride, of course!' said Anne. 'Do you see the mist rising over the water? It looks just like a veil, but then, I don't think I'll ever be a bride! Never mind, I'll spend my days helping you and Mrs Cuthbert on your farm.'

Matthew chuckled. Anne had not stopped chattering since the moment the horse had left the station. Everything was exciting and new to her.

'It's *Miss* Cuthbert,' Matthew corrected her. 'She's my sister. Neither of us are married, and we don't have children of our own.'

'I see,' said Anne, thinking for a moment. 'So that is why you need me. Well, I intend to learn all about farming and the countryside. You can rely upon that.'

Matthew stayed silent. Anne realised he was a man of few words.

The sun had almost set when they passed through the gates of Green Gables.

'Is *this* your home?' asked Anne, as though they had just crossed a moat into the grounds of a castle. When Matthew nodded, Anne's eyes filled with tears of joy. 'Oh, Mr Cuthbert, it is the most beautiful house I have ever seen! I feel like it is home already!'

Anne jumped down from the wagon. Her eyes took in the two-storey wooden house with the green-painted gables that had given it its name. It felt like heaven to her, and a million miles away from the orphanage she had just left in Charlottetown.

'Who's this?' asked a tall, thin woman. She was standing in the doorway to the house, wiping her flour-covered hands onto her apron. Her greying hair was pulled off her face in a tight bun.

'This is the child from the orphanage, Marilla,' said Matthew, a little uncertainly.

gable
A triangular bit of wall at the end of a ridged roof, often above a window or door.

‘But she’s a girl!’ answered Marilla, stepping down from the front porch to get a closer look. ‘We don’t want a girl, we want a boy.’

Anne's heart plummeted. All the excitement she had felt on her journey disappeared. The Cuthberts wanted a boy, and although Anne liked to imagine that her hair was brown or that her name was Cordelia, she could not imagine being a boy full time.

But now that she had seen Green Gables, she also could not imagine leaving it.

Chapter Three

Once inside the small kitchen of Green Gables, Marilla cut a slice of cake and placed it in front of Anne. 'Eat that while we figure out what to do with you,' she said.

Anne picked up her fork, the tears that had been building up inside starting to fall. 'You don't want me,' she sniffed. 'It makes sense. Nobody ever wanted me. It's probably because of my red hair ...'

Marilla blinked at this logic, but some of her sternness melted. 'There's no need to cry,' she said. 'We're not about to turn you out of the house tonight. You can stay here and we'll discuss it in the morning. And it certainly doesn't have anything to do with your hair.'

This comforted Anne a little, and she ate her cake in four big mouthfuls. Afterwards, Marilla showed her up to a bedroom. When Anne saw the small bed, wardrobe and desk, she was both thrilled and upset. She had never had a room to herself before and now here it was, but she did not know how long she would have it for.

Marilla helped Anne to unpack the few belongings she had, including a thin nightdress with holes that had been patched over many times. Anne settled into bed, feeling comfier than she had ever been. As Marilla blew out the candle and said goodnight, however, Anne's eyes filled with tears once more.

Back downstairs, Marilla reminded Matthew, 'The reason we wanted to take on an orphan was to help you on the farm. You aren't getting any younger, brother. What good would a little girl be to us?'

Matthew sighed, stoking the fire in their living room. 'Perhaps that is not the question we need to be asking,' he said. 'Perhaps we need to ask ourselves what good *we* could be for *her* ...'

Chapter Four

The Cuthberts' wagon rocked from side to side, jostling Anne and Marilla together. It was the following day and they were on their way to a nearby village called White Sands.

'I want a word with Mrs Spencer,' said Marilla, staring straight ahead as she drove the horse. 'I want to know why she ignored my instructions.'

Mrs Spencer was the woman

who had delivered Anne to the station where Matthew had met her. When the Cuthberts heard that Mrs Spencer was getting the train all the way to Charlottetown to collect an orphan girl, they had asked for an eleven-year-old boy for themselves. Marilla was annoyed that this well-made plan had gone wrong, but Anne had decided to be cheerful.

'I am going to enjoy this journey,' said Anne. 'I'm not going to think about going back to the orphanage. I'm going to admire the pretty flowers and that bright, shining pond.'

'If you're determined to talk,' said Marilla, 'why don't you tell me a bit about where you come from?'

'Well, I was born in Nova Scotia,' said Anne. 'Both my parents were teachers and very poor – although they loved me very much, so I have been told. They died when I was little, and no one knew what to do with me. At first, Mrs Thomas took me in to help with her own children. When Mrs Thomas didn't want me anymore, I went to work for Mrs Hammond. Mrs Hammond had *three* sets of twins – can you imagine? That was a lot of babies to look after! When she couldn't afford to feed me as well as all her children, I was sent to the orphanage.'

Marilla had taken her eyes off the road to look at Anne in shock. She did not know what to say, but she suddenly understood why Anne could find joy in simple things like flowers and ponds. It was because there had been so few other joys in her life so far.

Marilla was saved from having to think of a reply when the wagon trundled into White Sands. It stopped at a big yellow house.

'We're here,' said Marilla.

'Marilla Cuthbert?' said a voice. 'Whatever are *you* doing here?'

Chapter Five

The yellow house belonged to Mrs Spencer, but the curious voice did not. It belonged to a red-faced woman wearing a dirty apron.

'Hello, Mrs Blewett,' said Marilla, politely – although Anne could see in Marilla's face that she was not pleased to see her. 'I've come to speak to Mrs Spencer.'

'And who is this?' Mrs Blewett asked, eyeing Anne as they climbed down from the wagon.

'This is Anne,' explained Marilla. 'Mrs Spencer brought her back from Charlottetown for Mathew and I by mistake. We asked for a boy.'

'I'll take her,' said Mrs Blewett. 'I need help with the scrubbing and the cooking. I've too much on my hands as it is.'

Marilla glanced at Anne. The Blewetts were known for treating anyone who worked for them very badly. Maids were sent to

sleep in barns and they were never paid fairly.

'Oh hello, Miss Cuthbert,' said Mrs Spencer, appearing in her doorway. 'What can I do for you?'

Before Marilla could explain the situation, Mrs Blewett did it for her. At the end she said, 'So I am going to take the girl off her hands.'

'Perfect!' said Mrs Spencer.

'No!' said Marilla, suddenly standing in front of Anne like a bear protecting her cub. 'I mean … I'm terribly sorry, there has been some sort of misunderstanding,' she continued more calmly. 'Anne and

I were merely coming to see *how* the mix up had occurred, not to find a new home for her. Anne's just fine staying with us. Thank you very much.'

Marilla did not wait to see Mrs Blewett's reaction as she ushered Anne back onto the wagon.

'Good day!' called Marilla, shaking the reins and jolting the horses into a sudden trot.

Anne beamed. 'That was perfectly marvellous!'

'Well, I couldn't leave you with the Blewetts,' said Marilla, still a little flustered. 'But don't you go thinking you're going to have it easy with *us*, young miss. If you are to live with us, you will be brought up properly. You'll help around the house and you'll go to school.'

Anne nodded eagerly. She was not afraid of housework, and she had always wanted to go to school.

I'll be Anne of Green Gables, she thought. It made her so happy her heart could have burst.

Chapter Six

The following day, as Marilla and Anne were making bread together, Anne asked if there were any other children in Avonlea.

'Oh yes, many,' replied Marilla. 'You will meet them when school starts again. Our neighbours, the Barrys, have a daughter a little younger than you called Diana.'

Anne smiled.

'How wonderful,' she said. 'I have never had a real friend before – although I have had many imaginary ones. They kept me company while I did my chores at the orphanage.'

Marilla sighed and wondered how Anne could remain so cheerful when her life had been so sad and lonely. Marilla had never married, but at least she had always had her brother and her friends around her.

At that moment, a woman appeared

at the back door holding a basket of assorted fruit and vegetables.

'Oh, good morning, Rachel,' said Marilla, opening the door to let her in. 'Anne, this is Mrs Lynde. She is one of my oldest friends and she grows the best produce in Avonlea. Rachel, this is Anne, the orphan I told you we were getting.'

Rachel put her basket on the kitchen table and gaped at Anne. 'But it's a *girl*,' she said. 'And a funny looking one at that. Why, she's as skinny as my runner beans and her hair's the same shade as those carrots!'

Anne glared at Rachel. 'How dare you!' she shouted. 'That was a horrible thing to say! I hate you!'

While the women gasped in shock, Anne ran out of the door and into the fields behind Green Gables. An embarrassed Marilla was left to apologise to Rachel, who was not used to children – or *anyone* – talking back to her.

Anne ran and ran until she found Matthew working in one of the furthest fields on the farm.

'Whatever is the matter?' asked Matthew when Anne appeared. Her face was red from running and wet with tears. Bread dough still clung to her fingertips.

'That Mrs Lynde is a wicked woman!' said Anne.

Matthew simply nodded, as though no further explanation was needed.

Chapter Seven

That evening, after Rachel had gone home and Anne and Matthew returned from the fields, Marilla laid out the dinner in silence.

Matthew, who found angry women and girls the most frightening things on earth, summoned all his courage to speak. 'Now Anne, I think you owe Marilla an apology,' he said at last.

'She owes *Rachel* an apology,' argued Marilla.

'Rachel should say sorry to *me*!' said Anne.

Matthew sighed. 'Fine. Marilla, do you remember when you were young and the preacher's wife said you were plain-looking?'

Marilla glared at Matthew. 'I do,' she said, grumpily.

'You were sad for weeks after that so maybe you know a little about how Anne feels. And Anne,' Matthew continued. 'I may have only known you a short while, but I believe you know right from wrong. Do you think it was wrong to shout at Marilla's friend and say that you hated her?'

Anne nodded her head. 'Yes, I suppose it was,' she said. 'I'll go and apologise tomorrow.'

Matthew was so pleased with himself that he allowed himself a small smile, and finished his dinner in peace.

The next morning, Marilla took Anne to see Rachel. Anne had stayed awake all night thinking about what she had done. She might not like Rachel, but she was sad that she had embarrassed Marilla. The moment they arrived at Rachel's house, Anne launched into her apology.

'Mrs Lynde, I can never fully express my sorrow,' she said. 'Not if I used up a whole dictionary. I'm a dreadfully ungrateful girl.

I deserve to be cast out by respectable people like you forever.'

Rachel was so impressed with the young girl's words that she smiled in spite of herself. 'Well now,' she said when Anne had finished. 'Then I shall apologise for what I said, too. Now that I see it again, I think you have beautiful hair. Not like a carrot at all.'

That was enough for Anne. She stroked her pigtails and bit into one of Rachel's crisp apples, satisfied.

Chapter Eight

As Anne continued to settle in to Avonlea, she had her first chance to meet Diana Barry. Diana was small, with bright blue eyes and long, dark, shining hair. While Mrs Barry drank tea with Marilla, the two girls played outside.

The Barrys' garden was perfect for playing in. It had a long lawn, a swing set and a tree house. To Anne, it looked like a garden from a picture book, and Diana looked like a doll. Anne tried not to be jealous of Diana's pretty dress, with its flowery pattern and puffed sleeves. She did not want to be jealous of the girl who she had already decided was going to be her best friend.

'I would like to make you a proposition,' said Anne to Diana.

'What's that?' replied Diana.

'It means an offer,' explained Anne. 'I am offering to be your best friend, and you can be mine. I promise to be the most devoted friend you will ever have – I have had many imaginary friends before, so I have had lots of practice.'

Diana giggled. 'Yes, please!' she said. 'And if we are best friends, we can go to the Sunday school picnic together!'

Anne agreed, although the thought of going to the picnic filled her with dread. Anne found Sunday school boring, but the worst part was that all the other little girls always dressed in their finest clothes. Anne dressed in the same plain dresses Marilla had made for

Sunday school

A form of religious education. Usually, held on Sundays for young people at a place of worship, such as a church.

her when she first arrived at Green Gables.

The night before the picnic, Anne asked if she could borrow Marilla's pretty purple brooch to wear. Marilla always pinned it to her blouse on a Sunday, so Anne knew it must be special.

'Certainly not, child!' said Marilla, not looking up from her sewing. 'That brooch is one of the only things my mother owned that was precious. I can't have it getting lost at a picnic.'

Anne was sad, but she understood.

'In that case, may I take the chocolates Matthew gave me?' she asked. 'If I share my chocolates, no one will notice how plain my dress is.'

Marilla couldn't see what was wrong with Anne's dress, but she agreed about the chocolates, and Anne went to bed happy.

Chapter Nine

Marilla paced up and down the wooden porch of Green Gables. She was waiting for Anne to come home from the Sunday school picnic. She wrung a washcloth between her hands and tried to stay calm, though her anger burnt within her.

When the wagon pulled up in front of the house, Marilla said, 'Where is it? I know you took it.'

Anne and Matthew looked at

each other, then back at Marilla.

'My mother's purple brooch! I went to clean it this morning and it wasn't on my dressing table,' Marilla continued.

Anne shook her head. 'I'm sorry, Marilla, I don't know where it is. I didn't take it.'

'And now you're lying!' Marilla cried, her face red with anger. 'Go to your room and don't come out until you can tell me the truth!'

Anne was too shocked to argue. She ran up to her room and shut the door, tears filling her eyes. The picnic had been lovely. She had shared her chocolates and even next to Diana who wore a light blue party dress with lace trim, no one had mentioned the plainness of her own dress.

As day turned to night, Anne stayed in her room. She longed for some dinner but she had told the truth – she really *didn't* know what had happened to the brooch.

Eventually, she heard footsteps outside her door, followed by a voice.

‘I want you to tell me what you’ve done with my brooch,’ said Marilla, sounding a little calmer now but still stern. ‘If you don’t, I am cancelling our trip to the Barrys tomorrow.’

Anne jumped up from her bed. The best thing about Green Gables so far had been her friendship with Diana. She was determined to be friends with her for as long as she lived. Their outing simply *couldn’t* be cancelled. Diana might invite another friend over and then Anne would be forgotten.

Anne made a quick decision.

'All right!' she called. 'I did take your mother's brooch, but I lost it at the picnic. I'm sorry, Marilla!'

Anne heard Marilla let out a long sigh.

'Very well,' she said. 'You must stay in your room until the morning. Then we will go and visit the Barrys.'

Anne didn't like lying to Marilla, but telling the truth hadn't helped her. *At least this way I'll still get to see Diana,* she thought.

Chapter Ten

A disappointed Marilla brought a basket of laundry into the living room and began to hang it in front of the fireplace.

'I thought we were getting somewhere with Anne,' she said. 'Then she steals and *lies* about it.'

Matthew rubbed his chin, thoughtfully. 'It isn't like her,' he said. 'She might be a talker and a daydreamer, but she's not a liar.'

'Clearly we still don't know her

well enough to– Ouch!' Something sharp pricked Marilla's finger. She searched the folds of her Sunday blouse and gasped. It was her brooch! It was still pinned in place where she had left it at the weekend.

'Oh Matthew, look!' she said, showing him the brooch. 'What have I done?'

Marilla left the laundry. She piled a plate high with leftover dinner from the kitchen and rushed to Anne's room. 'Dear girl, I am so sorry,' she said, placing the plate on Anne's bed. Anne stared at the purple brooch in Marilla's hand.

'Why did you confess to taking it?' asked Marilla.

'Because I wanted to see Diana,' replied Anne. 'She promised we would have ice cream. I've never tasted ice cream before. I was worried that Diana would find a new friend to play with and I would have to go back to having imaginary friends again.'

Marilla fought back tears. 'Well,' she said. 'Now you don't need to worry. We will go to the Barrys and eat ice cream and never mention this again.'

Chapter Eleven

Anne was on her way to her first day of school, and she couldn't wait to start learning. She wanted to be as smart as her parents, who had been teachers, after all. She already loved to read. Even at the orphanage she would sneak books off shelves and hide somewhere for an hour or two to read them.

The Avonlea school was one big room in a wooden building. It had a bell to call the students in from the schoolyard, a large blackboard and rows of desks with a single piece of slate for each child to write on in chalk.

One of the best things about school, Anne discovered, was that she got to sit next to Diana every day. They even ate their packed lunches together under the willow tree and played jump rope in the playground before afternoon lessons.

Anne loved it there, until the morning a boy she didn't recognise walked in. He was a little older than she was, smartly dressed, and he seemed to be friends with everyone.

'That's Gilbert Blythe,' whispered Diana. 'He's been on holiday with his family.'

Anne rolled her eyes. 'He's making us all late for lessons.'

Gilbert had taken his time to find his seat, which happened to be right behind Anne. All the boys wanted to ask him questions about his trip, while all the girls stared at him adoringly.

'Hello, are you new?' asked Gilbert, leaning over his desk to talk to Anne.

'Yes, I am,' replied Anne. 'Now will you be quiet so the teacher can begin?'

Anne's classmates gasped. No one spoke to Gilbert Blythe like that!

As Mr Phillips began to write the day's lesson on the blackboard, Gilbert reached forwards and tugged one of Anne's pigtails.

'No need to be like that, carrots!' he whispered.

If there was one thing Anne hated to be called, it was "carrots". It had been bad enough when Rachel Lynde said her hair was the same colour. This time, her reaction was even worse.

Chapter Twelve

Anne saw red at the insult. She shot to her feet, grabbed Gilbert's writing slate and smashed it on the floor.

Gilbert looked at Anne with shock. The schoolroom fell silent.

'Anne Shirley!' Mr Phillips bellowed. 'Come here this instant!'

Anne immediately regretted what she had done. For the rest of the day, she was made to stand at the front of the class, all through lessons and all through lunch.

Anne's stomach grumbled as she spotted the paper bag that contained her packed lunch sat waiting on her desk. She shifted her weight from leg to leg to stop herself getting pins and needles.

'Here, take this,' whispered Gilbert, handing Anne a cracker.

'No, thank you,' said Anne, stubbornly.

'I'm sorry I got you into trouble,' Gilbert said. 'I was trying to make you laugh, but I shouldn't have called you carrots.'

Anne stayed silent.

'Please, take the cracker,' Gilbert tried again.

'No,' she replied. 'And I do not accept your apology. I should not have lost my temper, but I will never forgive you, Gilbert Blythe!'

Gilbert snuck back out of the schoolroom, and Anne's stomach grumbled again.

As the weeks continued, it became clear that Gilbert was not just popular – he was clever, too. He and Anne often came joint top of the class in spelling, maths and reading. It annoyed Anne so much that she vowed to one day be better than Gilbert at everything – even if it meant reading all the books in the Avonlea library twice.

Chapter Thirteen

One day, when Marilla and Mrs Barry were going out to run errands, Diana came to tea at Green Gables. Anne felt very grown-up as she set the table with Marilla's second-best tea set and a bunch of wildflowers in a glass vase.

It was the first time the two girls would be on their own, and Anne wanted the table to look just like a picture from one of Marilla's housekeeping books.

'Now, make sure you don't eat all of the cake, Anne,' said Marilla, buttoning up her coat and securing her hat to her head with a pin. 'Matthew will want some when he comes back from the fields this afternoon.'

'Yes, Marilla.'

Anne craned her neck to see if Diana and Mrs Barry were coming up the path. There they were!

Giggling with excitement, Diana and Anne waved goodbye to the grown-ups before taking their seats at the table.

'May I pour you some tea, Diana?' Anne asked, in what she thought was a very ladylike manner.

'You may,' replied Diana, copying Anne's tone.

The two girls did as they were told and left some cake for Matthew. They then played in the fields around Green Gables until they were both exhausted.

'I'm thirsty,' said Diana, as they collapsed on the porch. 'Tea is

nice and all, but my throat needs something cool.'

'We have raspberry cordial!' said Anne, jumping to her feet. 'Wait here.'

Anne searched the pantry to find the correct bottle, but she realised that she did not know which one it was. She had never seen Marilla pour the cordial before. And they all looked so similar.

In the end, Anne reached for a bottle of dark, red liquid that looked like it could be raspberry cordial. She poured two big glasses and took them out to the front porch.

Drinking raspberry cordial on the porch was not something Marilla would have approved of.

It was something farm hands did, not respectable young ladies, but Anne thought it would be OK just this once. The girls took a big gulp of the liquid, then looked at each other, wide-eyed.

'That doesn't taste like any raspberry cordial' Diana said, pulling a face.

'It tastes kind of … sour,' Anne agreed, taking another sip. 'Maybe it's gone off? I'd better take it back.' But as Anne reached for Diana's cup, she realised Diana had finished hers. 'I guess you *were* thirsty.'

Diana giggled. 'I still am to tell you the truth,' she said, taking Anne's cup out of her hand and finishing that one too.

Anne took the cups to the sink. When she returned to the porch, she saw that Diana had her head in her hands.

'Oh Anne,' she said pitifully. 'I don't feel so good ...'

Chapter Fourteen

Anne took Diana into the living room and laid her down on the sofa. She was devastated that the raspberry cordial had made her friend so poorly. As Diana drifted into sleep, Anne waited nervously for Marilla and Mrs Barry to return.

'What are you doing out here?' asked Marilla, as the cart and horse pulled up outside of Green Gables.

‘Oh dear, I’m afraid Diana drank too much of the raspberry cordial,’ explained Anne. ‘It must have been off because she’s now lying down on the sofa and not feeling very well.’

Marilla looked confused. ‘But we don’t have any cordial. We ran out last week,’ she said. ‘What on earth did you drink instead?’

Anne rushed into the kitchen to show Mrs Barry and Marilla the bottle. Mrs Barry’s face turned pale with worry and Marilla’s face turned pink with embarrassment.

‘That’s Matthew’s red currant wine!’ said Marilla.

The adults flew into the living room, where Mrs Barry scooped Diana off the sofa. ‘Look what you’ve given my little girl!’ she cried.

‘I’m sorry,’ Anne said, confusion and fear filled her mind. ‘I didn’t know!’

But Mrs Barry wasn’t listening. Diana looked very poorly indeed now. Matthew was called in from the farm to carry her to the wagon.

‘You will never play with Diana again!’ Mrs Barry said, as the wagon pulled away from the house.

Anne began to cry. Marilla turned to her. ‘Tell me one thing, and I will believe you,’ she said. ‘Did you know the bottle had red currant wine in it?’

Anne shook her head. 'As sure as I am standing here, Marilla, I promise you that I didn't.'

Marilla nodded and placed an arm around Anne's shoulders. 'Well then, we'll have to hope Mrs Barry believes that one day, too.'

Chapter Fifteen

Weeks passed and Anne was still not allowed to play with or speak to Diana. Mrs Barry had even asked Mr Phillips to change the school's seating plan so that the two girls were not sitting next to each other.

To distract herself from losing the first real friend she had ever had, Anne decided to focus all her energy on her schoolwork. Soon, she had read books that were meant for much older students and written several papers on history and geography.

Anne was working late on one of these papers at Green Gables when Diana burst through the living room door, her face stricken with panic. 'Oh, help me! You must help!'

Marilla was in Charlottetown with Rachel to attend a political meeting. There was only Matthew and Anne in the house.

'Whatever is the matter, child?' asked Matthew.

'It's Minnie, my little sister. She is sick and has a fever and Mama is out of town at that meeting and the babysitter doesn't know what to do!' Diana said, her voice rising with each word.

'It's all right,' said Anne, placing a calming hand on Diana's shoulder. 'I know just what to do. You didn't help to raise three sets of twins without learning a thing or two.'

Anne turned to Matthew and asked him to go and fetch a doctor. Then she ran to the pantry to fetch a bottle of medicine Marilla kept for emergencies.

'Let's go,' Anne said, and the two girls set off for the Barrys' home.

Minnie was just three years old, and her small body was red-hot with fever. Anne recognised the illness straight away as something called croup.

'She'll be all right, as long as we act fast,' said Anne. 'Fetch some cloths and soak them in cool water. Light a fire, but only a small one. I'll give her a dose of this medicine and plenty of water.'

croup

A disease that causes coughing and difficulty breathing.

The babysitter, a young woman from Avonlea, was a little shocked at first to be told what to do by an eleven-year-old girl, but she did as Anne instructed.

For the next few hours, Anne did not leave Minnie's bedside. By the time the doctor and Matthew arrived in the early hours of the morning, Minnie was sitting up and her fever had lessened.

As Matthew and an exhausted Anne prepared to leave, Diana gave Anne a big hug. Anne smiled. If they could not be friends, she was at least happy that she had been able to help.

Chapter Sixteen

'We have received an invitation,' said Marilla, a few mornings after Minnie had been taken ill. 'An invitation to go for tea at the Barrys.'

Anne almost spat out her breakfast. '*Truly?* When?'

'This very morning – so you had better run and put your best dress on!'

Anne rushed to her room and

put on her best dress. Today, she did not care that it was plain and did not have puffed sleeves like the other girls' dresses – she was going to see her best friend again!

The Barry's kitchen table had been laid out beautifully with the best china, fresh flowers and a whole plateful of cakes and biscuits.

'Mrs Barry, the table looks beautiful,' said Marilla. 'Surely, this is not all for us?'

Mrs Barry looked serious. She came closer to Anne and spoke in a soft voice.

'The doctor told me that what you did for Minnie saved her life. I owe you my thanks, Anne, and an apology. I am sorry I didn't believe you about the currant wine. I know now that you are a good, honest girl, and I hope this tea will help you to forgive me.'

Anne had never been spoken to in such a way by a grown-up. It made her feel ten-feet tall.

She smiled. 'There is nothing to forgive, Mrs Barry. As long as Diana and I can be friends again, I'll be as happy as can be!'

Anne could not believe how much had happened since she first arrived in Avonlea. She loved her new life, she loved her best friend and she loved the Cuthberts. Even if she had to spend the rest of her school days with Gilbert Blythe, it was worth it to be Anne of Green Gables.

Chapter Seventeen

Five Years Later

Over the years, Anne Shirley had grown into a clever, kind and hard-working young woman. She only had one year left at the Avonlea school and she was determined to enjoy herself.

As Anne and Diana entered the schoolroom and took their usual seats on the first day of class, they realised that Mr Phillips was no longer stood in his usual spot at the front of the class. Instead, there was a young woman.

'Good morning, class,' said the woman. Instantly, the chattering of the children hushed. 'My name is Miss Stacy. I am very pleased to be your new teacher. I hope that you are excited to start the new school year. Now, if you will all come along with me!'

With that, Miss Stacy flung open the doors of the schoolroom and went outside. This was something Mr Phillips had never done. Anne was the first to follow Miss Stacy. Gilbert was the second.

'Since I am new to Avonlea, I thought we ought to get to know each other,' Miss Stacy said. 'Let's play a game. If I catch you, you must tell me your name and one thing about yourself. If you catch me, you can ask me anything you like.'

The younger children squealed with delight and instantly began running around. Gilbert smiled at Anne, who, despite still being determined to dislike him, smiled back.

As the game continued, the children learnt that Miss Stacy's first name was Muriel. She was twenty four years old and she had a cat called Smudge. When the game finished, the children filed back into class and began their lessons without a single complaint.

Anne knew from that day that Miss Stacy was *everything* she wanted to be. She was intelligent, beautiful, funny and everyone liked her. For that reason, Anne did not mind a bit when Miss Stacy asked her to stay behind after school a few weeks later.

'Have you thought about what you will do when you leave school?' asked Miss Stacy.

'I am going to help run the Cuthberts' farm,' replied Anne. 'Matthew and Marilla are getting older and it is time I helped.'

'Have you ever thought about

going to college?' asked Miss Stacy. 'You are the cleverest girl in the school. You could be a teacher one day if you worked hard and got some qualifications.'

Anne's eyes grew wide. 'A teacher?' she said.

Miss Stacy nodded. 'I am going to put both you and Gilbert forward for the entrance exam to Queen's College.' Miss Stacy handed Anne a small, folded piece of paper with the Queen's College picture on the front. It was a grand building with ivy creeping up the walls. To Anne, it seemed as distant as a princess's castle, one that belonged in a fairy tale.

Chapter Eighteen

The fire crackled as Marilla, Anne and Matthew sat comfortably in each other's silence after dinner. Marilla was sewing and Matthew was mending a fishing rod. Anne was re-reading the folded piece of paper Miss Stacy had given her. She already knew that she would not be able to go. College cost a lot of money.

'I had a visit from your teacher the other day,' said Marilla, not looking up from her sewing. 'She thinks you are good enough to go to Queen's College in Charlottetown.'

'It is a kind suggestion, but I know I cannot go,' said Anne.

'And why not?' said Matthew. 'Aren't you the cleverest girl that school has ever seen?'

Anne's cheeks flushed. 'It isn't that,' she said. 'I can't *afford* to go. It's OK. Just knowing that Miss Stacy believes I am good enough is enough for me.'

Marilla put down her needle and thread and shared a small

smile with Matthew. 'Anne, we have known for some years now that you have a bright future. You are too clever to spend your days helping me milk the cows. We have been saving a little money here and there and we have enough to send you to college.'

Anne couldn't believe it. Although she had come to see Green Gables as her home, she always knew that the Cuthberts were not her parents. She had only ever called them by their first names. But now they were offering to pay for her to go to college.

‘I … I don’t know what to say,’ Anne said at last.

‘Well, that will be a first!’ laughed Marilla.

‘There is nothing to say,’ said Matthew.

‘When we took you in all those years ago,’ said Marilla, ‘I made a promise to myself to bring you up the best way we could. We are so proud of how far you’ve come, now it’s time to see how much further you can go.’

Anne jumped up and hugged Marilla, who, despite still not being used to such affection, hugged her back. Of all the places Anne's imagination had taken her, college had seemed the most fanciful. Now the dream was coming true, and she had to pinch herself to believe it.

Chapter Nineteen

There were only two things wrong with Queen's College: the first was that Diana was not there, and the second was that Gilbert was.

Gilbert had also been accepted into Queen's College with Anne. In fact, they had scored the *exact* same mark on their entrance exam.

Anne stood at the large wooden door to the grand building that housed Queen's College. She glanced down at her dress and smiled. Matthew had managed to persuade Marilla to buy Anne a new dress at last, rather than making one from the same old plain material as her others. She felt prettier than she ever had.

Anne pushed open the door and found her way to the correct classroom. It was much larger than the one at Avonlea school and Anne wished she knew someone in the crowd. Then, she saw Gilbert.

Gilbert waved, but Anne took her seat next to a girl in a blue checked dress.

'How do you do,' Anne said, cheerfully. 'I'm Anne. Pleased to meet you.'

'I'm Josie Pye,' the girl replied. 'Are you as nervous as I am?'

'I don't believe in being nervous,'

Anne said. 'I never thought I would be somewhere like this, so I am going to treat every day as a gift.'

Although nobody would ever replace Diana in Anne's heart, Josie and Anne soon became good friends. Josie was fun and already knew a lot of people in the college. One lunchtime, a girl called Ruby joined them.

'Ruby and I went to school together,' said Josie.

'Have you girls heard the news?' said Ruby. 'They are going to give a scholarship out at the end of the year to the student with the best grades!'

'A scholarship for what?' asked Anne.

'To pay for university of course!' said Ruby. 'My Gilby told me about it. He's going to try out for it. If you go to university, you could become a doctor or a lawyer …'

'Who's "Gilby"?' Josie asked with a giggle.

'Gilbert Blythe! He's very handsome and very smart,' said Ruby. 'Anyway, I have to go!'

Ruby dashed out of the lunch hall leaving Anne with two things on her mind. The first was the scholarship. If she won it, she would carry on learning for another three years, for free. The second, and why she felt so annoyed, was when Ruby called Gilbert Blythe "my Gilby".

Chapter Twenty

Anne's year at Queen's College flew by. She learnt a great deal, and she grew up a lot too. She did not daydream as much anymore, and things like dresses and afternoon tea were not so important to her. She had even grown to like her red hair.

She remembered telling Josie how she did not believe in feeling nervous. It felt like such a foolish thing to say, because Anne was *very* nervous now. The end-of-year exam results had been posted on the board just outside her classroom. Anne was trying to summon the courage to look.

Finally, she made her way through the crowd of students and found the list. She was top of the class! Gilbert's name was right below hers. She had beaten him at last.

'Congratulations, Anne,' said a voice behind her. It was Gilbert.

'Thank you,' said Anne. 'And well done to you, too.'

'I always knew you were

smarter than me,' he laughed. 'And now you'll be going to university! The Cuthberts will be so pleased.'

Anne blushed. Despite how badly she had treated Gilbert in the past, he was still able to be kind to her.

'Well, I had better get going,' said Gilbert. 'Ruby will be waiting for me.'

Anne's smile faded a little as she watched Gilbert leave.

On her way home to Avonlea, Anne spotted a familiar face on the train. It was Rachel. Over the years, she had grown almost as fond of Anne as the Cuthberts had.

'I always knew you'd make something of yourself,' Rachel said, when Anne told her about the scholarship.

'Even when I shouted and said that I hated you?' replied Anne, remembering the day they first met.

Rachel chuckled. 'Well, maybe not at that moment! But I'm proud of you now – and I know Marilla and Matthew will be too.'

Chapter Twenty One

Marilla walked around the kitchen at Green Gables, preparing dinner. It had struck Anne that since being home, Matthew looked greyer in the face and had been spending more time in bed.

'Marilla, is Matthew feeling OK?' asked Anne, concerned.

'It's his heart, Anne. The doctor wants him to stay in bed and rest because he won't spare himself a minute. Maybe he will rest now you're home. You always cheer him up.'

Worry welled in Anne's stomach. She couldn't imagine a world where Matthew was bed-bound. At least she was home to spend time with him now and help out on the farm.

Anne, too, couldn't help but notice how much slower Marilla moved these days. She had started wearing thick glasses, but she still struggled to see things as clearly as she once did.

Anne had been telling Marilla

all about the university scholarship.

'That sounds wonderful, dear,' she said, placing a bowl of soup in front of Anne.

That evening, Anne lay in her bed in her old bedroom, unable to sleep. The scholarship was a wonderful opportunity, but she knew in her heart that she could not accept it. Matthew's health weighed on her mind, too.

Marilla and Matthew had taken her in all those years ago, even though she was not the boy they were expecting. Now it was time for Anne to repay the favour. She would stay at Green Gables and help them.

'But you can't give up your scholarship!' said Marilla the next morning when Anne told her that she was not going to go to university.

'I can and I will,' said Anne. 'I heard that Miss Stacy is leaving the Avonlea school to get married, so I thought I could take her position. I can work as a teacher and help here in the mornings and evenings.'

Marilla sat down at the kitchen table. She looked tired even though the day had just begun. 'I'm afraid Gilbert Blythe has already taken

Miss Stacy's position,' she said.

Anne rolled her eyes in spite of herself. 'Then I will work at another school,' she said. 'But one thing is for sure: I am staying here at Green Gables.'

Chapter Twenty Two

Anne worked at the little desk in her bedroom. First, she wrote a letter to Queen's College and turned down her scholarship. Then, she made a list of all the schools in the area and wrote to each one with a list of her qualifications and exam results. Within a week she had a reply from a school in a town called Carmody. It would take her an hour to get there each day, but she would still have time to help on the farm if she got up extra early. Until the school year started, she could help out every day.

A few days later, Anne was bringing in a pale of milk from the cow shed when she noticed a familiar figure walking down the path towards Green Gables. Her stomach tightened and her face flushed a little. It was Gilbert.

Quickly, Anne took off her apron and straightened her hair. She did not want Gilbert to see her looking like she had spent the morning in a barn – even though that is exactly what she had done.

'Good afternoon, Gilbert,' said Anne as calmly as she could when Gilbert reached the front porch. 'What brings you to Green Gables?'

'It is good to see you, Anne. You may have heard that I've been given the teaching post at the Avonlea school.'

'I have,' replied Anne.

‘Congratulations.’

‘I want *you* to have it instead,’ replied Gilbert. ‘And I will take your post at Carmody.’

Anne was unable to speak, which was very unlike her.

'I heard you were giving up the scholarship to stay close to the Cuthberts,' Gilbert continued. 'It doesn't make sense to spend all that time travelling when you could be helping out here.'

'Thank … thank you, Gilbert,' said Anne at last. She was trying hard not cry with happiness. 'That is so kind of you.'

Gilbert smiled. 'Perhaps now we can stop being enemies and start being friends?' he suggested.

Anne laughed. 'Yes,' she said. I believe we can be good friends.'

Anne held her hand out towards

Gilbert, inviting him to shake it. He gently took her hand in his. At last, Anne decided to forgive Gilbert for pulling her pigtails all those years ago. He had grown into a kind man, and had given her the chance to teach and stay close to the Cuthberts at the same time.

As they stood next to each other, Anne realised Gilbert still had hold of her hand. For the first time in her life she felt total and complete happiness, and excitement of what was to come.

Lucy Maud Montgomery

Lucy Maud Montgomery was a Canadian author born in 1874. Montgomery studied English Literature becoming one of the few women of her time in higher education. In 1905, she wrote *Anne of Green Gables*.
It was unsuccessful for several years, until Montgomery resurfaced the manuscript from a hat box and decided to send it to a publishing house once more. In 1908 it was published and became an immediate success.